DERRYDALE BOOKS
New York/Avenel, New Jersey
Copyright © 1992 by Peter Haddock Ltd, England
All rights reserved.
This 1992 edition is published by Derrydale Books.
distributed by Outlet Book Company, Inc.,
a Random House Company,
40 Engelhard Avenue
Avenel, New Jersey 07001.

Printed and Bound in Singapore

ISBN: 0-517-08667-0

8 7 6 5 4 3 2 1

PUSS IN BOOTS

Retold & Illustrated by John Patience

There was once a miller who was very poor and when he died all that remained for his three sons were his mill, his donkey and his cat. The eldest son took the mill, the second the donkey and the youngest had nothing but the cat.

"My brothers have done well," said the youngest son to himself. "If they get together they can make a living with the mill and the donkey, but what is to become of me?" "Don't be sad, master," said the cat. "Just give me a sack and have a pair of boots made for me and you will soon see that you have a better bargain than either of your brothers."

The miller's son was very surprised to hear the cat talk. "A cat that can talk may be clever enough to do as he promises," he thought. So, with the little money he had, he bought a pair of beautiful leather boots and the cat put them on. "Well now, Puss in Boots, what are you going to do?" asked the young man. "Wait and see," replied the cat and he swung a sack over his shoulder and set out into the woods.

The cat hid himself by a rabbit warren and soon tricked a silly young bunny into his bag. Then off he went to the king's palace. Once there, he demanded to see the king and was escorted into the throne room. "Your Majesty," he said, "I have brought you a present from my master, the Marquis of Carrabas." This was the title he had invented for the miller's son.

When he saw that the king was pleased with the rabbit, Puss caught other small creatures, such as hares and partridges, and gave them to the king, pretending that they all came from the Marquis of Carrabas. Naturally, the king began to feel very friendly towards the strange nobleman.

Now one fine day the cat heard that the king and his daughter, the most beautiful princess in the world, were going to take a drive by the riverside. So Puss went to his master and said, "You are in luck today. Just bathe here in the river and leave the rest to me!"

While the miller's son was bathing, the royal coach came by and the cat began to shout, "Help! Help! My master, the Marquis of Carrabas, is drowning!" Seeing that it was the cat who brought him gifts, the king ordered his royal guards to save the marquis. "Thank you, Your Majesty," said Puss, "but what shall my poor master do now, for a thief has stolen his clothes?" The king was very sorry to hear this and at once offered the young man a suit of fine clothes. And when the miller's son was dressed in these rich clothes he looked every inch a marquis and the princess immediately fell in love with him.

The king then invited the miller's son to ride with them back to the palace, so the young man stepped into the carriage and sat beside the princess. Meanwhile the cat hurried on ahead. He stopped when he reached a meadow where a couple of mowers were working and he called out to them, "The king is coming this way. Tell him that this meadow belongs to the Marquis of Carrabas. Do this or I'll have you chopped up as fine as mincemeat!" The mowers were so frightened by the cat's fierce face that they did as they were told and Puss hurried on and ordered the reapers, ploughmen and woodcutters to do the same.

The king was amazed by the great lands owned by the Marquis of Carrabas!

Now the fields really belonged to an ogre
who lived in a nearby castle. Puss knew
about the ogre and called at the
castle door.

"Sir," said the cat, "I have been
told that you are able to turn yourself into an elephant
or a lion." "Indeed, I can," said the ogre proudly.
And the next moment he transformed himself into a
great lion and let out a terrible roar which shook the
castle walls. The cat was so frightened that he
scrambled up on to the top of a high cupboard.

After a while, the ogre changed himself back into his own form and Puss jumped down again. "Well," said the cunning cat, "that was very fine. But I have also heard it said that you can take on the shape of a tiny creature, such as a mouse. I am sure that is quite impossible." "Impossible!" growled the ogre. "Why, nothing is impossible for me!" And in the blink of an eye, there was a fieldmouse scampering around the floor. With one leap the cat caught the mouse and gobbled him up. And that was the end of the ogre!

Meanwhile, the king had seen the castle and decided to pay a call on its owner. The coach rolled up to the castle door and waiting there was Puss in Boots. "Welcome to the castle of my master, the Marquis of Carrabas!" he called. The king was delighted to hear that his friend lived in such a splendid castle.

The young man invited the king and the princess into the great hall, where a feast had already been prepared by the ogre for his friends. Fortunately they did not arrive. When they had finished eating, the king declared that, since the marquis and the princess had obviously fallen in love, they ought to get married. This they did and lived happily ever after. As for Puss, he lived off the fat of the land until the end of his days!